TIME SWITCH

White Wolves Series Consultant: Sue Ellis,
Centre for Literacy in Primary Education

This book can be used in the White Wolves Guided Reading
programme for independent readers in Year 5

First published 2007 by
A & C Black Publishers Ltd
38 Soho Square, London, W1D 3HB

www.acblack.com

ISBN 0-7136-8135-7
ISBN 978-0-7136-8135-2

A CIP catalogue for this book is available from the British Library.

This book is produced using paper that is made from wood grown
in managed, sustainable forests. It is natural, renewable and
recyclable. The logging and manufacturing processes conform
to the environmental regulations of the country of origin.

Printed and bound in Great Britain by MPG Books Limited.

TIME SWITCH

Steve Barlow & Steve Skidmore

Illustrated by Sue Mason

A & C Black • London

Contents

Historical note

The first Globe Theatre was built
in 1599 in London on the south
bank of the Thames near Southwark
Cathedral. It was built for one of the
best companies of actors in England
– the Lord Chamberlain's Men. The
company's chief writer was William
Shakespeare. It was here that many
of Shakespeare's most famous plays
were first performed.

Characters

Bev   A stage-struck girl

Tim   Her friend

Hayley   Her friend

Wat   A child actor

Old Jill Wat's mother

William Shakespeare

The action of the play takes place in the Globe Theatre in London, in the present day and in the year 1600.

Act One

The stage of the Globe Theatre – present day.

It is night. The stage is dark. **Bev, Tim** *and* **Hayley** *come on.* **Bev** *is carrying a rolled-up poster.* **Tim** *carries a torch.*

Tim Is this the right place, Bev?

Bev Of course it is! Don't you recognise the Globe Theatre when you see it?

Tim I can't see *anything* – it's dark!

Hayley (*stamping her feet*) And it's *freezing*.

Bev You two are such wimps! I've brought you to the most famous theatre in the world, the theatre where William Shakespeare himself performed, and all you can do is moan.

Tim (*sulking*) It's not the original Globe – it's only a copy.

Bev It's the same size and the same shape and it's roughly where the real theatre used to be...

Hayley What are we doing here anyway?

Bev Oh, Hayley, give me a break – I told you. I'm here for an open audition...

Hayley Audition?

Bev Don't you *ever* listen? I'm going

to read for a part in a play.

Hayley Why's it 'open'?

Bev It means anybody can turn up.
(*She unrolls the poster.*) Tim – shine
that torch over here, will you?

Tim (*grumbling*) I still don't see why me and Hayley have to be here…

Bev To give me moral support. Now, can I have less moaning and more shining.

Tim *shines the torch on the poster.*

Bev See? (*Reading.*) Open audition for the Original Shakespeare Company, the Globe Theatre, Bankside, London, 7 pm.

Hayley *takes the poster and looks at it closely.*

Hayley Why's it in that funny, old-fashioned writing?

Bev How should I know? Maybe they wanted it to look like a proper Elizabethan playbill.

Tim It looks shut to me.

Bev The poster?

Tim The theatre. It's all dark and there's nobody about. Are you sure you've got the right day?

Bev Of course I'm sure.

Hayley (*waving the poster*) Hey – there's something printed on the back.

Bev Let's see. (*She reads.*) It looks like a couple of lines from one of Shakespeare's plays – I think it's *A Midsummer Night's Dream...* We did it at drama club.

Tim Read it out, then.

Bev (reading) 'Now you shall but slumber here

    While these visions do appear...'

Instantly the stage is filled with light.
Actors (including **Shakespeare***) are*
reading their lines out loud. Stagehands
are carrying props and costumes about.

Tim What's happening? Where did
this lot spring from?

Bev These must be people who've
come for the audition.

Wat *enters, pulling a costume hamper*
across the stage. He bumps into **Hayley**,
who squeals.

Wat (*rudely*) By your leave, mistress.

Wat *drags the hamper off.* **Bev**, **Tim**
and **Hayley** *stare after him.*

Hayley What did he say?

Tim (*thoughtfully*) If these people
have come for an audition, they've

gone to a lot of trouble. They're all wearing Elizabethan clothes...

Bev That's not fair! It doesn't say anything on the poster about turning up in period costume. I've only got jeans and a sweatshirt.

Hayley There's something weird going on. I don't like it.

Bev Calm down. I'm sure there's a perfectly simple explanation. I'll ask that bloke over there.

She crosses the stage to where **Shakespeare** *is rehearsing his lines.*

Shakespeare 'Two households, both alike in dignity
    In fair Verona, where we lay our scene...'

Bev Excuse me...

Shakespeare (*irritated*) Anon. (*He reads the lines again.*) 'Two households, both alike in dignity

In fair *Verona*, where we lay our scene...'

Bev (*tugging at his sleeve*) Excuse me...

Shakespeare 'Two households, both alike in dignity

> In *fair* Verona...'

Bev Excuse me!

Shakespeare (*breaking off*) By the mass, what would'st thou? (*He stares at the girls' clothes.*) Od's boddikins, thou art strangely attired! Art thou a comedian?

Hayley (*nervously*) What's he saying?

Bev (*to* **Hayley**) That's how they used to talk in Shakespeare's time. He wants to know what we want, and he says we're wearing strange clothes.

Tim Look who's talking!

Hayley He's a weirdo.

19

Bev (*to* **Shakespeare**) Listen, I'm here for the audition. I am in the right place, aren't I?

Shakespeare Audition? Marry, art thou wandering in thy wits?

Bev There's nothing wrong with my wits – I mean, I'm not crazy! I've come for the audition – see?

She waves the poster in front of **Shakespeare**'s *nose.* **Shakespeare** *gives a startled exclamation and grabs the poster from her hand.*

Shakespeare Aha! I am amazed, and know not what to say! Thou art not from this time!

Bev What do you mean?

Tim I'm getting a very bad feeling about this.

Bev Look, I don't know what's going on. I've just come for the audition – why is everybody dressed up? And who are you?

Shakespeare (*bowing*) William Shakespeare, mistress – at your service.

Bev Yeah, right. Well I'm Florence Nightingale, and my friends here are Bart Simpson and Minnie Mouse.

Shakespeare Your servant, Mistress Nightingale.

Hayley He *is* a weirdo.

Bev Will you stop saying that?!

Tim Hang on a minute – you said we weren't from this time. What year is this?

Shakespeare Why – 'tis the Year of our Lord, 1600.

Bev I've heard of people living their parts in a play, but this is ridiculous. You can stop pretending now, all right? You're not Shakespeare, you're just an actor, and this isn't the year 1600, it's...

Tim Sssh! Hear that?

Bev What? I can't hear anything!

Tim Exactly. Where's the traffic? You can always hear traffic in London. And trains. And planes. I can't hear anything...

Hayley Oo-er.

Bev Don't you start! This can't be 1600 – that's over four hundred years ago. It's impossible.

Shakespeare I assure you, mistress, I speak truly. This is the year 1600, Good Queen Elizabeth sits upon the throne of England, and you are in the Globe Theatre, home of the Lord Chamberlain's Men.

Tim You mean, this really *is* the Original Shakespeare Company? Are you telling us we've travelled in time?

Bev (*to* **Tim**) You're cracked!

Shakespeare Not so, mistress –
thy friend Bart is in the right. You
have been brought here by magical
arts.

Tim (*in a panic*) That's terrible! I
can't stay here! 1600? It's the Dark
Ages! They haven't got microwave
pizzas or MP3 players or television!
They don't even have *electricity*!

Hayley I want to go home!

Shakespeare Fear not, Mistress
Mouse. (*He looks around.*) This is too
public a place for all that must be
said. Follow me to yon tiring room.
(*He leads the way offstage.*)

Hayley What's a tiring room?

Bev It's where they keep the
costumes.

Shakepeare Come, my friends. Let truth make all things plain. For these are grave times. Both this company and this theatre stand in terrible danger – and only you can save us!

Act Two

The tiring room of the Globe Theatre in the year 1600.

The room is cluttered with costumes and props. **Bev**, **Hayley** *and* **Tim** *are sitting on hampers.* **Shakespeare** *is pacing about.*

Bev All right, so what's this danger? And what do you think *we* can do about it?

Shakespeare Hast thou heard of the Black Death?

Tim Yes. It's a disease. If you get it,

you come out in a red rash...

Hayley Yeuch!

Tim And then you get horrible swellings full of pus in your neck and under your armpits...

Hayley Yeeeuuuch!

Tim And then you get headaches and start sneezing and after that, you usually die.

Bev Trust you to know about things like that!

Tim It's interesting! The Black Death was a big thing in Elizabethan England. Thousands of people were killed…

Hayley That's terrible!

Tim And if you had the plague in your house, you had to put a red cross on the door and you were locked in…

Hayley I think I'm going to faint.

Tim And then the death cart would come round and they'd shout, 'Bring out your dead!' and they'd take the bodies away and throw them in a pit, where they rotted away and smelled and...

Bev Too much information, Tim! (*To* **Shakespeare**.) It all sounds very nasty, but what's it got to do with you? Or us?

Shakespeare The plague is a terrible curse. Not long ago, all the theatres were closed down.

Bev Right, that *is* serious! But this theatre isn't closed now, is it?

Shakespeare No. But, alas, it might as well be!

Bev I don't get it.

Shakespeare Wherever a crowd gathers, plague may strike.

Tim And there's always a crowd at the theatre.

Shakespeare Thou sayest sooth.

Tim What do I sayest?

Bev He says you're right. (*To* **Shakespeare**.) So?

Shakespeare We have no young actors. Many have died. Those who still live avoid the theatre, like... like...

Tim Like the plague?

Shakespeare Verily! Our company contains only greybeards...

Bev (*to* **Tim**) Old duffers. (*To* **Shakespeare**.) All right, I see the problem. But how does all this explain how *we* got here?

Shakespeare Well, Her Majesty…

Hayley Queen Elizabeth.

Shakespeare As you say, Queen Bess – commanded us to play *Romeo and Juliet* for the court. Alas, I had to tell her that we could find no one to play Juliet.

Tim I bet she went ballistic.

Shakespeare (*puzzled*) What sayest thou?

Tim I said, I bet she did her nut. Went bananas. Threw a wobbler. Lost her rag. Hit the roof.

Shakespeare *is completely baffled.*

Bev He means, she wasn't pleased.

Shakespeare Aye! Marry, she was not. But Her Majesty is a lady of strong will and she sent for Doctor John Dee.

Hayley Who's he?

Shakespeare John Dee is Her Majesty's chief magician.

Hayley (*shocked*) You mean, the queen believes in magic?

Bev Hayley, this is four hundred years ago. *Everyone* believed in magic.

Tim I told you it was the Dark Ages.

Shakespeare Her Majesty put our problem to Doctor Dee – and he found the answer!

Tim And what was that?

Shakespeare He ordered a playbill to be written...

Hayley *looks down at the poster she is still holding in her hand.*

Hayley You mean, this poster?

Shakespeare ...and on it, he cast a most potent spell...

Hayley *drops the poster as if she has been burnt.*

Shakespeare ...that anyone who read aloud the words set upon it should be brought by magic here to the Globe, to be our Juliet.

Bev (*dramatically*) And the magic has worked! I'll be your Juliet!

Shakespeare *gapes at* **Bev**, *speechless with shock.*

Tim What? What are you talking about? We can't stay here!

Bev But this is too good a chance to miss! I've always wanted to be on the stage.

Hayley But Bev, we're four hundred years in the past. We don't belong here...

Bev *I* do! Just think – it's the chance of a lifetime – I'm going to act with

William Shakespeare...

Shakespeare (*recovering his voice*)
Mistress, are you mad?

Bev What? But you said...

Shakespeare *You* cannot play Juliet!

Bev (*angrily*) Why not? Don't you
think I'm good enough? You haven't
even heard me read...

Shakespeare It boots not.

Tim He says, it doesn't matter.

Bev I understood what he said!
(*To* **Shakespeare**.) Why doesn't it?

Shakespeare Thou art a wench.

Tim He says you're a girl.

Bev Tim, will you shut up? (*To*

Shakespeare.) Yes, I'm a girl – well spotted. So? What's that got to do with anything?

Shakespeare A wench cannot appear on the stage!

Bev Why not?

Shakespeare 'Tis unheard of! If we allowed such a thing, the royal officials would close us down at once!

Bev That's sexist!

Hayley Hang on – are you saying that women aren't allowed on stage?

Shakespeare 'Tis even so.

Hayley Er – I'll take that as a 'yes'. So – who plays the girls' parts?

Shakespeare Why – boys, of course.

Bev (*with deep disgust*) *Boys*?!

Shakespeare Aye. 'Tis the custom.

Bev Well, it's a really stupid custom if you ask me. (*She stands up.*) This is a waste of time! You drag us four hundred years into the past, looking for someone to play Juliet...

Hayley Yeah!

Bev And I say I'll play Juliet, and you're not interested. Fine! Send us back...

Shakespeare Tarry, mistress.

Tim I think he wants us to wait.

Shakespeare 'Tis true that thou cans't not play Juliet. But thy friend, Master Bart...

Bev Oh for goodness' sake, that

was a joke, his name isn't Bart, it's Tim. (*She suddenly realises what* **Shakespeare** *has just said.*) *Tim*?!

Shakespeare Aye, marry, Master Tim, if that be his true name.

Tim (*to* **Shakespeare**) Now, hold on…

Bev You want *Tim* to play Juliet?

Tim (*to* **Shakespeare**) Now, just a minute…

Bev You don't want me, you want *Tim*? *Tim*, who couldn't act his way out of a paper bag?

Tim (*to* **Shakespeare**) Exactly! (*He realises what* **Bev** *has just said about him.*) Eh?

Bev *Tim*, who's got a face like a

warthog's bottom?

Tim (*to* **Bev**) Now, look...

Bev *Tim*, who wears clothes that a Guy Fawkes' dummy wouldn't be seen dead in?

Together:
Tim Excuse me!
Shakespeare Who is Guy Fawkes?

Bev *Tim*, who has about as much personality as a toothbrush?

Tim I've had enough of this! I don't want to play Juliet – but if I *did*, I bet you I could!

Shakespeare Excellent! We must find thee a costume... (*He rummages in a hamper.*)

Bev (*to* **Tim**) All right! Prove it.

Tim (*worried*) Well, when I said 'could'...

Bev Put up or shut up.

Shakespeare *finds a nightgown and passes it to* **Tim**.

Shakespeare Here, put this on.

Tim Er...

Hayley (*giggles*) Oh, go on, Tim. I bet you'll look lovely!

She helps **Tim** *into his costume.*

Tim No! Get off! I feel stupid...

Bev (*nastily*) Not half as stupid as you look.

Shakespeare *finds a wig and passes it to* **Hayley**.

Shakespeare Here!

Hayley *puts the wig on* **Tim** *and steps back.*

Hayley You know, Tim – if I was a bloke, I could quite fancy you.

Tim (*miserably*) Thanks very much.

41

Shakespeare Thou art the image of Juliet! Now, let us be about our business. Thou must rehearse thy part. To the stage!

He leads **Tim**, *still protesting, out of the tiring room.*

Tim Look – I can't… I'm not well, I've got a note from my mum, I have nose bleeds, I've got a verruca…

Bev (*to* **Hayley**) Come on – this, I must see!

They follow the others out.

Act Three

*The stage of the Globe Theatre in the
year 1600.*

Shakespeare *comes on, dragging the
reluctant* **Tim**. **Bev** *and* **Hayley** *follow.*

Shakespeare Here, Master Tim,
here is thy place. And here is thy
side.

He passes **Tim** *a roll of parchment.*
Tim *looks at it.*

Tim What's this?

Shakespeare It's a list of the
speeches thou must make as Juliet.

Tim Don't I get a copy of the full script?

Shakespeare (*laughs*) Hear him! Master Tim, there is only one full copy of the play. Dost thou think we have an army of scribes, to write it out for everyone?

Tim But how do I know what the other characters are going to say?

Shakespeare Thou wilt *hear* what they say. What more would you?

Bev That's how they used to do it, Tim. You only get your own part.

Shakespeare And I shall read the part of Romeo. We will begin with the balcony scene. Art ready?

Tim Er...

Shakespeare (*reading*) 'But soft!
What light through yonder
window breaks?
It is the East, and Juliet is the
sun!'

Tim (*reading – very nervous*) 'Oh
Romeo, Romeo! – wherefore art thou,
Romeo?'

Shakespeare Master Tim, thou
soundest like a bullfrog croaking at
the bottom of a well! Thou art
supposed to be a young maid.

Bev *and* **Hayley** *giggle at* **Tim**, *who is
starting to feel a fool.*

Tim Young maid. Right, right. Young
maid. (*Reading again in a high voice.*)
'Oh Romeo, Romeo! – wherefore art
thou, Romeo?'

Shakespeare Now, thou soundest like a cat with its tail caught in a door!

Bev *and* **Hayley** *fall about laughing.*

Shakespeare Perhaps something in between…?

Tim (*finding his 'Juliet' voice*)
'Oh Romeo, Romeo! – wherefore
art thou, Romeo?'

Shakespeare Thou has it!
Excellent!

Wat *comes on carrying a basket of
props, including a property dagger.*

Wat Master Shakespeare, where
would you like me to...?

Shakespeare Anon, Wat, anon.

Shakespeare *goes into a silent
conversation with* **Tim,** *explaining with
excited gestures how he wants him to
play the part of Juliet.* **Wat** *notices* **Bev**
and **Hayley,** *and scowls at them.*

Wat What is Master Shakespeare
about with that onion-eyed knave?

Bev What's it to you? Who are you anyway?

Wat Wat.

Bev I said, who are you?

Wat Wat!

Bev (*to* **Hayley**) He must be deaf as well as ugly.

Hayley Um – Bev...

Wat Wat is my name!

Bev That's what I just asked *you*!

Wat By this hand, thou mockest me!

Bev What?

Wat What?

Bev (*to* **Hayley**) Is it just me, or is he talking complete rubbish?

Hayley I think he's trying to tell you that his *name* is Wat.

Bev Well, why didn't he say so in the first place?

Wat Fie upon thee! I did say so...

Shakespeare 'Zounds, peace! You scold like fishwives! Mistress Nightingale, Mistress Mouse, if thou canst not hold thy tongues...

Bev (*pointing at* **Wat**) He started it!

Shakespeare Enough! Get thee to the tiring room – there are costumes to be sewn.

Bev Costumes? You want us to sew costumes?

Hayley Oo-er – come on, Bev, we don't want any trouble...

Bev (*furious*) You're wasting your time trying to make Tim into an actor. I've *played* Juliet, you slap-headed twit! (*Dramatically*.) 'The quality of mercy is not strained…'

Tim That's not Juliet, that's Portia. In *The Merchant of Venice*.

Bev (*unconvincingly*) I knew that.

She allows **Hayley** *to drag her to the side of the stage.*

Wat Master Shakespeare – what is this whey-faced lout doing here?

Shakespeare Guard your tongue, boy. Master Tim is here to play Juliet.

Wat But you said *I* could play Juliet!

Shakespeare I did not!

Wat You said if I was the last actor of my age left in England...

Shakespeare But thou art not the last actor of thy age left in England! By happy fortune, Master Tim has arrived to play Juliet.

Wat But what of my triumph in *A Midsummer Night's Dream*? My Bottom was the talk of London.

Bev (*nastily*) It's big enough.

Wat I mean, my role as Nick Bottom the Weaver. Audiences were amazed by my ass's head...

Bev ...and the ass's brain inside it.

Wat The audience clapped and cheered when the Queen of the Fairies fell in love with me, in the form of a donkey...

Bev ...and no mask needed! Well done!

Wat A plague upon thee, wench!

Shakespeare Fie! I'll have no more wrangling. (*To* **Wat**.) Thou canst not play Juliet.

Wat Why not? Tell me that!

Shakespeare Because thou art ugly and spotty and thou canst not remember thy lines. I had rather a bear played Juliet than thee!

Bev *is doubled up in laughter.*

Wat Would you make a fool of me?

Shakespeare Fie, fie! As thou art here, thou canst read Romeo.

Shakespeare *hands the part he has been reading to* **Wat**, *who takes it but continues to sulk.*

Shakespeare Now, from 'Deny thy father...'

Tim (*as Juliet*) 'Deny thy father and refuse thy name.
    Or, if thou wilt not, be but sworn my love
    And I'll no longer be a catapult.'

Bev That's 'Capulet', you div!

Tim 'And I'll no longer be a Capulet.'

He stops and looks expectantly at **Wat***, who reads Romeo's lines in a dull, flat voice.*

Wat 'Shall I hear more, or shall I speak at this?'

Tim (*starting to enjoy himself*) ' 'Tis but thy name that is my enemy.
          What's Montague? Oh, Romeo, doff thy name
          And for thy name, which is no part of thee
          Take all myself.'

Wat (*sulkily and without expression*)
'I take thee at thy word.
          Henceforth I never will be Romeo.'

Tim 'What man art thou?'

Shakespeare And now – Romeo kisses Juliet.

Tim No way!

Shakespeare Hah? What sayest thou?

Tim I'm not kissing him!

Shakespeare But thou lovest him!

Tim I don't think so!

Shakespeare I mean, *Juliet* loves him!

Bev She must have pretty low standards.

Glowering, **Tim** *kisses the air at least a metre away from* **Wat**'s *face, then goes back into role as Juliet.*

Tim 'Goodnight, goodnight! Parting is such sweet sorrow

That I shall say goodnight till it be morrow.'

There is a moment's silence.

Shakespeare Perfect! Wonderful! Thou art our Juliet!

Wat (*angrily*) And what am I?

Shakespeare Thou shalt have the role of third servingman, and think thyself lucky!

Wat (*in a rage*) Then *this* for thy Juliet! Speak, hands, for me!

Wat *siezes a property dagger from the props basket and stabs* **Tim** *with it.* **Bev** *gasps.* **Hayley** *screams.*

Shakespeare No!

There is a moment's silence. **Tim** *and* **Wat** *do not move. Then* **Wat** *looks puzzled, withdraws the dagger and stabs* **Tim** *again.*

Tim *does not react.* **Wat** *stabs* **Tim** *some more. Nothing happens.* **Tim** *holds out his hand.* **Wat** *presses the dager against* **Tim***'s palm. The blade slides into the handle.*

Hayley (*relieved*) It's a trick dagger!

Shakespeare S'blood, Wat! Art mad? Wouldst thou murder this youth because he has a part thou didst want for thyself? Out upon thee! Thou art fired!

Wat *drops the dagger and goes. He turns at the door.*

Wat I'll be revenged on the whole pack of you!

Hayley Oo-er. I don't like the sound of that.

Bev Oh, don't worry. He's all mouth.

Shakespeare Very well, Master Tim. We will take a short break. Wilt join me in a cup of ale?

Tim Yes, I wilt – sorry, I mean, I will, Will.

They go off.

Hayley Now what do we do?

Bev You follow that Wat bloke and see what he's up to. I'm going to have a word with the lovely Juliet.

They go off.

Act Four

The tiring room of the Globe Theatre in the year 1600.

Tim *is sitting on a hamper, learning his lines.*

Tim 'Goodnight, goodnight! Parting is such sweet sorrow!'

Bev *enters.*

Bev What do you think you're doing?

Tim I'm learning my lines. My Juliet will go down in history!

Bev Only because it will be so bad! Where's Mr Slap-head gone?

Tim Mr *William Shakespeare* has gone to the tavern to get me a tankard of ale.

Bev But you're too young to drink!

Tim That's what I told Will, but he said that water is too dangerous to drink. It can kill you! So everyone drinks ale!

Bev Well, never mind that, what do you think you're up to? You can't seriously go ahead with this Juliet stuff.

Tim Why not?

Bev For a start, you're not a girl.

Tim So? I'm getting in touch with

my feminine side.

Bev If you don't stop this nonsense, my foot will get in touch with your backside.

Tim You wouldn't be moaning so much if Shakey had chosen you to play Juliet.

Bev (*hesitantly*) I would...

Tim Oh no, you wouldn't...

Bev Oh yes, I would...

Tim Oh no, you wouldn't...

Bev Oh yes, I... Oh shut up! This isn't a pantomime.

Tim Well, admit it. You'd love to play Juliet. 'A chance of a lifetime', you said. Well, this is *my* chance of a lifetime.

Bev But you don't like acting! How can this be your chance of a lifetime?

Tim Because this is my chance to make you *soooo* jealous and get one up on you. It'll probably never happen again!

Bev Look, Tim, this is crazy. We shouldn't be here! It's not right! We've got to think of a way to get back to our own time and you're not helping...

Tim Maybe I don't want to go back home. I'm beginning to enjoy it here. Just imagine: the smell of the greasepaint, the roar of the crowd. I'm going to be a star!

Bev You're going to be dead, if I get hold of you.

Bev *makes a grab for* **Tim**. *He dodges her. As* **Bev** *tries to catch* **Tim**, **Shakespeare** *enters with two tankards of ale.*

Shakespeare What ho! You men, you beasts! Cease this caterwauling! Come, Master Tim, I have refreshment for us.

He hands **Tim** *a tankard.*

Tim Cheers! (*To* **Bev**.) I don't get this at home!

Shakespeare Let us go forth to yonder stage and rehearse another scene, my Juliet!

Tim Righto!

Bev 'My Juliet?' Yeuch!

Shakespeare (*to* **Bev**) And, Mistress Nightingale, I thought I told thee to stop dilly-dallying and be about thy business.

Tim (*to* **Bev**) Yes, Mistress Nightingale, stop dilly-dallying and be about thy business.

Tim *and* **Shakespeare** *head off to the stage.*

Bev (*under her breath*) I'll be about thy business in a minute. (*Shouting.*) Tim! Come back here!

She follows **Tim**. *As she exits,* **Hayley** *enters from the opposite side.*

Hayley Bev! Tim! We're in big trouble! Wat's gone bonkers. He's steaming mad, he's…

She hears **Wat** *shouting from outside.*

Wat (*very angry*) I will make worm's meat of them!

Hayley Oo-er!

Wat When I see them, I will cut an equal pound of their fair flesh!

Hayley Oh no!

She hides behind a hamper as **Wat** *enters. He is with his mother,* **Old Jill**.

Wat I will do such things – what they are yet I know not; but they shall be the terrors of the earth!

Old Jill Wat, my son, forsooth. Be still. You are too hot.

Wat (*angry*) They have wronged me, Mother. I should be Juliet.

Old Jill And so thou wilt be, my boy, so thou wilt be.

Wat How? Shake-rags has chosen some puny, flap-mouthed varlet to play Juliet.

Old Jill Am I not known as Old Jill the Wise Woman?

Wat (*under his breath*) Only to thyself. Old Jill the Mad Witch is what everyone else calls you.

Old Jill What sayest, Wat?

Wat Nothing, Mother. But how can it be that I may play Juliet?

Old Jill *takes a small bottle from her purse. She holds it in front of* **Wat**'s *face.*

Old Jill Poison!

Wat Poison!

Hayley (*from behind hamper*) Poison!

Wat *looks around.*

Wat Didst thou hear a noise?

Old Jill I heard the owl scream and the crickets cry.

Wat During the day?

Old Jill Or it could have been a mouse.

Wat A big mouse, methinks. How came you by this deadly potion?

Old Jill I made it in my bubbling cauldron.

Wat *looks carefully at the bottle.*

Wat What's in it?

Old Jill 'Eye of newt, and toe of frog,
    Wool of bat and tongue of dog.'
Oh no, that's what we had for dinner.

Wat You said it was soup.

Old Jill It was. Newt, frog, bat and dog soup. Beggars can't be choosers. And you'll end up as a beggar, if you do not remove this rival of yours.

Wat What should I do?

Old Jill Is there not a scene in the play where Juliet has to drink a sleeping potion?

Wat Aye. Friar Laurence gives it to her. She drinks it and falls asleep, but her family thinks she is dead.

Old Jill Then all thou hast to do is swap this bottle of poison with the one Juliet will drink from.

Wat (*realising*) And when this upstart Tim drinks it... (*He clicks his fingers.*) Dead!

Old Jill And you will be Juliet!

Hayley *has heard enough. She jumps up from her hiding place.*

Hayley No! You can't! It's murder!

She rushes for the door.

Old Jill Stop her!

Wat *grabs hold of* **Hayley**, *who struggles furiously.*

Hayley Get off me! Help! Murder! Bev! Tim! Anyone...

Hayley's *cries are cut off as* **Wat** *puts his hand over her mouth.*

Wat Be still, wench! (*To* **Old Jill**.) What should we do with her, Mother?

Old Jill Lock the wench in the hamper. We can deal with her later.

Wat *puts the struggling* **Hayley** *into the hamper, closes the lid and locks it.*

Hayley (*inside the hamper*) Help!

Old Jill Come, let us do a deed of dreadful note.

Wat What if we fail?

Old Jill Screw up thy courage. We will not fail. Come, Wat, thy rival shall soon be dead, and thou shalt be Juliet.

Wat *and* **Old Jill** *exit. As they do,*

Bev *enters from the opposite door. She is annoyed and wrapped up in her thoughts.*

Bev 'Off the stage and back to your sewing!' he says. 'Back to your sewing!' Just wait until I get Tim away from that shiny-headed buffoon!

Hayley Murder!

Bev Exactly! I'll murder him.

Hayley Poison!

Bev Yeah, nice idea, poison would work... (*She does a double take.*) Who said that?

Hayley Me!

Bev Me?

Hayley No, not you, me! Hayley,

Bev (*looking around*) Where are you?

Hayley In the hamper.

Bev What are you doing in there?

Hayley Waterskiing. What do you think? Stop asking stupid questions and get me out of here!

Bev *unlocks the hamper.* **Hayley** *gets out.*

Bev What's going on?

Hayley Tim's going to be murdered!

Bev No, I didn't mean it. I just said I wanted to murder him, 'cos I'm angry with him.

Hayley No, not by you, Wat.

Bev What?

Hayley Don't start that again!

Wat and his mother are going to
murder Tim. I overheard their plan.

Bev What plan?

Hayley They're going to swap a real bottle of poison with one of the prop bottles, and when he drinks it...

Bev Dead! Ah, well, it could be worse!

Hayley How?

Bev It could be you or me.

Hayley Bev!

Bev Well, he ruined my chance to play Juliet and there are an awful lot of costumes to sew...

Hayley Bev! Don't be horrible! Anyway, if Tim's murdered, the future might change. We might be stuck here for ever.

Bev How?

Hayley Well, he'll be dead before

he's alive and so he would never have met us and we would never have met him and then we wouldn't be here, so he couldn't be here and so... (*She runs out of steam.*) Oh I don't know, but it'll be bad if he dies.

Bev It will be for him...

Hayley And for us! Do you want to spend the rest of your life sewing costumes? We've got to get back to our own time.

Bev How?

Hayley Have you got the poster? (**Bev** *produces it.*) Maybe if we repeat the incantation, it will work in reverse and send us back.

Bev (*shrugs*) Might be worth a try.

Hayley Have you got a better idea?

(**Bev** *shakes her head.*) Come on, first we've got to stop Tim being poisoned and then get back home!

She rushes out, followed by **Bev**.

Act Five

*The stage of the Globe Theatre in the
year 1600.*

Tim *is rehearsing with* **Shakespeare**.
Wat *and* **Old Jill** *hover in the
background.*

Shakespeare Now, where were we?
Ah yes, Act Four, Scene One. Now, I
am Friar Laurence, and I am about
to give thee the potion that will make
thy family think that thou art dead.

Tim The potion. Right. Am I
frightened?

Shakespeare Aye, marry.

Tim *acts frightened – he goes completely over the top, trembling, sobbing, wringing his hands, etc.*

Tim Oh, woe is me! Alas! Alack!

Shakespeare Mayhap, not quite that frightened. Art ready?

Tim *nods.* **Shakespeare** *goes into character as Friar Lawrence.*

Shakespeare 'Take thou this vial...' (*He searches his clothes.*) Vial, vial... Where is that wretched vial? I knew I had forgot something.

Wat *comes forward, carrying a small bottle.*

Wat Here's a vial for thee, Master Shakespeare.

Shakespeare Wat! Did I not sack thee?

Wat Indeed, master. But I cry you mercy. I do repent of my folly and murderous rage.

Shakespeare Well – thankee, Wat. I shall speak more to thee anon. Now, Master Tim, to our scene.

Tim *goes back into overacting mode as Juliet, and* **Shakespeare** *repeats Friar Lawrence's line.*

Shakespeare 'Take thou this vial...
        And drink it off; through all thy veins shall run
        A cold and drowsy humour...'

Tim (*as Juliet*) Come, vial.

He takes the cork out of the bottle and holds it up.

Tim (*as Juliet*) 'Romeo, Romeo, Romeo!

> Here's drink. I drink to thee.'

He holds the bottle to his lips. **Bev** *and* **Hayley** *burst in.*

Bev Tim! Don't drink that! It's poison!

Shakespeare S'blood! Shall we never be free of interruptions? Mistress Nightingale, what would you?

Bev That stuff in the bottle – it's poison.

Shakespeare Marry, 'tis not. 'Tis a most cunning potion made by the good Friar to make it seem that Juliet is dead...

Bev I'm not talking about the potion in the play – I'm talking about the stuff in that bottle!

Wat The wench is mad!

Tim Bev, will you pack it in?

Bev What?

Tim You'll do anything to stop me

playing Juliet, won't you?

Bev What?

Tim You're just trying to scare me so I won't want to play Juliet any more.

Bev Listen, you bone-headed...

Tim You're just jealous of my acting ability.

Bev Your...? (*She is speechless.*)

Tim Forget it, Bev. It's not going to work. You're not playing Juliet. I am.

Bev Fine! Take the potion! See if I care!

Hayley Bev! No!

Bev You heard him! It's not my fault – I tried to warn him! He wouldn't listen.

Hayley Tim, Bev's telling the truth. Wat put poison in that bottle.

Shakespeare Ha! What sayest thou?

Wat 'Tis a lie!

Hayley His mother made a horrible potion of frog wool and newts' toenails and dogs' breakfasts, and all that sort of stuff, and they put it in that bottle so you'd drink it.

Old Jill *sneaks off.*

Shakespeare (*to* **Wat**) What foul deed is this, sirrah?

Tim *stares in horror at the bottle in his hand.*

Tim I nearly drank that!

Wat Marry, and shall!

Wat *leaps forward, knocking* **Shakespeare** *to the ground.* **Wat** *grabs the bottle and tries to force the contents down* **Tim**'s *throat.*

Wat Traitor, thou diest!

Tim Help! Get him off me! He's gone ravin' mad!

Bev *drops the poster and wrestles with* **Wat. Hayley** *goes to her aid.*

Bev Never mind Wat! Get the poster! Read the lines...

Hayley *picks up the poster and unrolls it. She turns it over and reads...*

Hayley 'Now we have but slumbered here
       While these visions did appear...'

Instantly the stage darkens. **Shakespeare** *and* **Wat** *disappear. Traffic noises can be heard.*

Hayley Did it work?

Bev *and* **Tim** *get to their feet and look around.* **Tim** *is still holding the bottle of potion.*

Bev Well – I guess it did. Wat's gone – and so has Shakespeare – and I can hear cars...

Hayley It worked! We did it! We're back in our own time!

Tim *is staring at the bottle in his hand.*

Bev (*to* **Tim**) Are you all right?

Without speaking, **Tim** *pours the poison from the bottle onto the ground. Where it lands, the ground smokes.*

Tim It's eating a hole right through the floor!

Bev Good job you didn't drink it. You should've believed me.

Tim Sorry, Bev.

Hayley Hard luck, Tim.

Tim Eh?

Hayley Well, I mean, you'll never get to play Juliet now. Do you mind?

Tim Not really. I don't think I'm cut out to be an actor – it's too dangerous. I think I'll take up skydiving or kick boxing or something instead.

Hayley How about you, Bev? Still want to work with William Shakespeare?

Bev You're joking! He's such a bloke! (*She imitates* **Shakespeare**'s *voice*.) Gadzooks and 'zounds, we cannot have women on the stage, by'r lady and out on't...

Hayley So you don't mind?

Bev No – I'm glad to be back. They

may be a bit bitchy in my drama club, but at least they don't try to poison you!

Hayley So – all's well that ends well.

Bev Well – not really.

Looking at **Tim**, *she whispers something into* **Hayley**'s *ear.* **Hayley** *doubles up with a fit of giggles.*

Tim What? (**Hayley** *and* **Bev** *are laughing too much to answer.*) What?

Bev Oh, nothing. It's just that... well, we could have a bit of fun getting home.

Tim Getting home?

Hayley Yes – people might give you some funny looks.

Tim Funny...?

Hayley When you go on the Tube, dressed as Juliet.

Tim *looks down at his Juliet costume.*

Tim Oh, no!

Bev Never mind – you can just tell them you're getting in touch with your feminine side.

Laughing so much they have to hold each other up, **Bev** *and* **Hayley** *leave the stage.* **Tim** *is left alone, looking around. He fingers the material of his costume, sadly.*

Tim I'd have been a great Juliet, though. I bet you.

Bev (*calling from offstage*) Come on, Tim!

Tim Coming!

He follows the girls off.

For a moment the stage is empty. Then, from the darkness, we hear **William Shakespeare**'s *voice.*

Shakespeare Next!

The End

About the Authors

Steve Barlow and Steve Skidmore have been writing together since 1987, producing over 90 books for children including stories, plays and non-fiction, including the *Lost Diaries*, *Dark Forest* and *Outernet* series.

Steve Skidmore lives in Leicester and supports Leicester Tigers RFC, Steve Barlow lives in Somerset and enjoys sailing. When they aren't writing they spend a lot of time traveling the country, visiting schools, libraries and festivals to talk about their work. They get their ideas from Ideas R Us and they don't want to get a proper job, thanks, because they're having too much fun.

Other White Wolves playscripts...

FOOL'S GOLD

David Calcutt

Prospero's had a dream – at last he's
going to discover how to turn ordinary
metal into pure gold. So when a pair
of tramps turn up at his door, telling
him they have a rare stone that will
give him this power, he jumps at the
chance to buy it. But surely things
aren't as simple as that?

Fool's Gold is a humorous Tudor play
with parts for five people.

ISBN: 9 780 7136 8138 3 £4.99

Other White Wolves playscripts...

Let's Go to London!

Kaye Umansky

A random group of travellers
meet on the riverbank one morning,
all heading for London town. But when
the ferryman is too drunk to take them
across the river, there's only one thing
for it – they must walk! Little do
they know what an adventure it
will turn out to be!

Let's Go to London! is a humorous
Tudor play with parts for six people.

ISBN: 9 780 7136 8151 2 £4.99

Year 5

The Path of Finn McCool • Sally Prue

The Barber's Clever Wife • Narinder Dhami

Taliesin • Maggie Pearson

Fool's Gold • David Calcutt

Time Switch • Steve Barlow and Steve Skidmore

Let's Go to London! • Kaye Umansky

Year 6

Shock Forest and Other Stories • Margaret Mahy

Sky Ship and Other Stories • Geraldine McCaughrean

Snow Horse and Other Stories • Joan Aiken

Macbeth • Tony Bradman

Romeo and Juliet • Michael Cox

The Tempest • Franzeska G. Ewart